Paperback ISBN: 978-1-952425-04-2
Hardcover ISBN: 978-1-952425-03-5
All rights reserved. Published by Jackal Moon Press.

A Spot of New

Written by
P. Anastasia

Illustrated by
Zoe Saunders

Hello there, friend.

How do you do?

I'm glad you're here. It's nice to meet you.

You must be brand new; your coat is bare.

There's not a spot here and not a dot there.

How would you like to glisten and gleam?

Shimmer and shine?

Sparkle and beam?

The first thing you do is choose where to start.
Don't think too hard, just follow your heart.

Paths bend and weave and intertwine.
There's no right answer and no straight line.

So much to do and you're already late.
Hurry along; don't make the world wait.

Take the first step and be on your way.
Adventures await you, starting today.

Who could that be?
Tall, dark, and hairy!

It may be a monster!
Big, mean, and scary!

It was only a shadow cast on the wall.
That tiny creature is no monster at all.

Don't make assumptions about the unknown.
You shouldn't judge others on looks alone.

Your very first friend! Two's better than one.
They climb on your back and you go for a run.

Bright colored berries hang overhead.
Purple, pink, and delicious dark red.

Your friend takes one first. Would you like a bite?
I think you should try it, and like it you might.

No way. Not a chance.
You simply don't buy it.

Then you give in
and decide to try it.

Nibble.

Bite.

Chomp.

That wasn't so bad.
In fact, it was tasty.
Next time, be patient
and not quite so hasty.

A spot, a dot, right there on your side.

You've certainly earned it. Now wear it with pride.

You're doing great! You tried something new.
Unfamiliar, at first, but that didn't stop you.

Let's keep on going. There's more to explore.
The future is filled with colors galore.

A stream blocks the way, but you must persevere.
If you don't cross now, the journey ends here.

You're not a fish. You don't know how to swim.
How will you learn, if you don't hop in?

Hooray! You're so brave! You've gained a new mark!

You're learning things and you're finding your spark.

Sometimes, you'll stop at a bump in the trail,
or a wall that's too tall, and plans start to derail.

Don't give up hope.
You will make it through.

If you can't go around,
up and over works, too.

Whoosh! You've got wings! Now you can fly!
You'll gallop and glide straight through the sky.

Soar to the moon, the stars, and the sun.
Paths have been opened. The fun's just begun.

Oh, no!
Seems your friend won't be tagging along.
High in the clouds is not where they belong.

They're frightened of heights, and that is okay.
Up you will go, and down they will stay.

It's sad to part ways, and everyone cries.
You smile and hug as hope glints in your eyes.

Goodbye, for now.
This isn't the end.

They'll always be there.
A friend is a friend.

You travel by morning, by day, and by night.

You travel by sea, by land, and by flight.

Who's that in the shadows, just out of sight?
Are they lost in the darkness, alone without light?

What if they're scared and in need of a friend?
You stretch out your wings and begin to descend.

Hooves touch the ground as you land with great care.

The little one's head tilts up...
and they stare.

They squint and they blink, their eyes small and gray.
"You sparkle and shine like a rainbow," they say.

"Hello," you reply, "how do you do?
I'm glad you're here. It's nice to meet you."

"A grand adventure is long overdue.

You'll soon have your very own spot of new, too."

ABOUT THE AUTHOR:

Kentucky author and voice talent, P. Anastasia has loved horses since childhood.

She has written two children's books and nine young adult novels, including *Morning Puppa*, *Exile of the Sky God*, the *Fluorescence* series, *Fates Aflame*, and *Dark Diary*.

Anastasia's unique take on storytelling springs to life with whimsy, charm, and a little bit of magic. She hopes this story inspires you to chase your dreams.

ALSO BY P. ANASTASIA

Morning Puppa

Written By
P. Anastasia

Illustrated By
Zoe Saunders

Use this page to color in your very own Spot of New.
(Color it any way you like!)

CPSIA information can be obtained
at www.ICGtesting.com
Printed in the USA
LVHW071946200922
728862LV00018B/662